Please re

You may

You can re

or Γ

TH.

JST BITE

Titles in Teen Reads:

Badger Publishing Limited, Oldmedow Road, Hardwick Industrial Estate, King's Lynn PE30 4JJ
Telephone: 01438 791037

www.badgerlearning.co.uk

JUST BITE

TOMMY DONBAVAND

Just Bite ISBN 978-1-78147-951-3

Text © Tommy Donbavand 2014
Complete work © Badger Publishing Limited 2014

Publisher: Susan Ross
Senior Editor: Danny Pearson
Publishing Assistant: Claire Morgan
Copyeditor: Cheryl Lanyon
Designer: Bigtop Design Ltd

2 4 6 8 10 9 7 5 3 1

CHAPTER 1

DELIVERY

The doorbell rang.

"Sally!" Mum shouted upstairs. "Can you get the door? It'll be dinner!"

I pulled off my headphones and sighed. She'd done it again – ordered food from that stupid Just Bite website instead of cooking. Another greasy takeaway. No wonder my skin was exploding with spots. I couldn't remember the last time I'd eaten a home-cooked vegetable.

I was halfway to my bedroom door when a thought struck me. "Why can't Mark get it?" I shouted. "He's already downstairs."

"He's getting the trays from the kitchen."

"And what about you?"

"I'm getting the drinks ready!"

The doorbell rang again.

"Hurry!" shouted Mum. "We don't want him taking it back to the restaurant."

"Restaurant!" I scoffed under my breath as I slowly made my way down the stairs. I'd seen some of the places with Just Bite stickers in their windows in town – and they were hardly what could be described as restaurants. Dirty burger bars and oily kebab shops – yes. Restaurants – no.

But that didn't put Mum off ordering from them, night after night. "Look at the choice!" she'd exclaimed when she first logged on to the website after seeing the TV ad. "I could have a Thai meal, while you and Mark get a pizza from the same place!"

So that was it. Pots and pans sat gathering dust in the kitchen while we kept the grimy takeaway shops of our town in business single-handedly.

It's been this way ever since Dad left, to be honest. He was never what you would call an inquisitive eater. Food was fuel to him. Fuel that enabled him to get through a day at work, a night at the pub and – more often than not – a roll in the hay with one of his many girlfriends before finally staggering home.

Since Mum had kicked him out (not before time!), she'd eaten anything but the beef stews or egg and chips my Dad had preferred. I'd laughed the first time she'd tried a really spicy curry. Her face was a picture – flushed with a mixture of spices and delight, tears rolling down her rosy cheeks. Like all those years putting up with Dad's bland taste buds were finally worth it.

But now it was getting out of hand...

The doorbell rang for a third time.

"Yes, yes," I called. "I'm coming…"

I pulled open the door, and there he was – clutching a padded red bag, his moped parked at the end of the drive.

Carlos!

My heart sank.

"Sally!" he beamed, running his fingers through his lank hair. "I wondered if this might be your house – what with the order being for Hagen. Not too many of them around here. Trust me, I've checked the phone book."

"Hi, Carlos," I said, reaching out for the food. He held the bag away.

"So this is where you live!" he said, stepping back to take it all in. "I'd never have found you all the way out here."

"That was the plan," I pointed out.

He dragged his eyes away from the front of the house and looked me up and down. "You look great without your school uniform on!"

"I beg your pardon?"

His face turned as red as the bag in his hands. "I mean – you look really nice in what you're wearing today. Your clothes, I mean."

"Yeah, I get it," I said.

I wished I could say the same for Carlos. He was dressed in a pair of trousers that were at least two sizes too large – pulled tight at his waist by a ragged leather belt. Tucked into that was a T-shirt featuring a bizarre character from some stupid science-fiction TV show I'd never be caught dead watching.

Was it any wonder he was picked on at school?

"Black," he said, obviously determined not to give up on the compliments any time soon. "It's a good colour on you."

"I like it."

"Mysterious… traditional, but with a hint of the night…"

"Are you going to give us our dinner, or do you just want to stand here talking about what I'm wearing all evening?"

"What? Oh, yes… here you go…" He ripped open the Velcro fastening on the bag and pulled out a handful of boxes. Too many for me to hold.

"Do you want me to bring them in for you?" asked Carlos.

"No chance!" I said, suddenly feeling mean as his face fell. "That is – not when I've got an annoying little brother to carry stuff for me." I turned towards the living room and yelled, "Mark, get your lazy butt out here and help me!"

"I'm watching telly!" came the reply.

"And I'm ready to tell Mum about those magazines you keep under your bed!"

My eleven-year-old brother was beside me in a flash. He looked at Carlos and frowned. "Isn't he that oddball who follows you around the corridors at school?"

One dead leg later, Mark was limping back towards the living room, carrying an assortment of takeaway boxes.

"OK, thanks," I said, starting to close the door.

Carlos put his hand against the wood to stop me. "Actually, there's something I want to ask you, Sally…"

I sighed. Here we go again… "Look," I said. "You're a really nice guy and all that, Carlos. I just don't know if I'll even be going to the prom, let alone with a date or anything. But, if I do decide to go, I'll definitely keep you in mind."

"Oh," said Carlos, swallowing hard. "Thanks. That's great. But I was just going to ask if I could nip to your loo?"

"I'm not sure that would be a good –"

"Of course you can!" interrupted Mum, appearing behind me.

I glared at her. "Really?"

"Thank you!" smiled Carlos, hopping from foot to foot. "It's a long drive back into town. I had a large Coke before I set off and I don't know if I'd make it back…"

"Well, don't stand out there in the cold," said Mum. "Come in!"

Nervously, Carlos stepped into the hallway. "There?" he asked, pointing to the door of the downstairs toilet.

"All yours!" said Mum.

Carlos disappeared inside with a grateful grin. I shook my head and turned towards the living room.

"Where do you think you're going?" Mum asked.

"To get my dinner."

"Don't be so rude!" Mum scolded. "Stay here and see your friend out when he's finished."

"He's not my friend!" I hissed.

"He's obsessed with her!" called Mark from the living room.

"You can shut up – unless you want another dead leg!" I shouted.

"Well, he seems like a nice lad to me," said Mum. "And you're not exactly swamped with boys asking you to the end-of-year prom, are you? Not since you started dressing like a depressed banshee…"

I struggled to keep my temper under control.

"I'm not having the clothes conversation with you again," I said. "I'm almost sixteen. I can wear what I like."

Mum raised an eyebrow. "Of course you can, dear," she said. "It's just that I've seen pandas with less black around the eyes…"

Before I could reply, the toilet flushed and Carlos emerged. "That's better!" he said. "Think I'll make it back without any accidents now!"

I opened the front door.

"Bye, Sally!" said Carlos, holding out his hand. It was wet.

I didn't move. Carlos lowered his hand and stepped outside.

"Right, then… see you at school on Monday!"

"I'm sure you will," I said, closing the door and breathing a sigh of relief.

"Cool!" shouted Mark from the living room. "They gave us free garlic bread!"

CHAPTER 2

DINNER

Mark was lying along the sofa, taking up all three cushions.

"Shift!" I said, trying to squeeze on the end.

"There's no room!" he whined. "Sit somewhere else…"

I looked around the room. There wasn't anywhere else. Aside from the sofa and Mum's armchair, there was a dining table – but that was piled high with clean washing, ready to be ironed and put away.

Gone were the days when we sat there and ate as a family.

So it was either the floor – again – or… I spun one of the dining chairs around and sat on it, facing into the room. I grabbed the two remaining boxes from the arm of the sofa to see what Mum had ordered for me.

Four pieces of fried chicken and a portion of chips covered with cheese. I could almost hear my arteries screaming for mercy.

"Kitchen towel?" said Mum, handing over a length of absorbent tissue instead of cutlery. So we were expected to eat with our fingers again, then.

"Don't get any grease on that clean washing!" she warned as I balanced my dinner on the edge of the table. There was a third box already there – the free garlic bread. I felt the fumes sting my eyes.

"I thought you wanted this…" I said to Mark.

He shook his head. "Can't stand the stuff," he said through a mouthful of mixed kebab.

"But I heard you shout 'Cool! Free garlic bread!'" I pointed out.

"Anything free is cool," Mark said. "Doesn't mean I have to like it."

I slid the stinking box as far away as I could and reached for the TV remote. It wasn't there.

"Oh, no!" I snapped, prying the remote from Mark's grasp. "It's my turn to decide what we watch."

"No, it isn't!" Mark protested, gripping the other end of the remote tightly.

"It is!" I said. "You made us sit through an hour and a half of Wolf-man cartoons last night!"

Mark grinned. "Oh yeah…" He let go of his end of the remote.

"Somebody pick something, or I will," said Mum, settling into her armchair with a tin tray of something bright red and steaming. "And I know neither of you are particularly keen on those home makeover shows I like."

I shuddered at the thought and flicked through the TV programmes recorded on our system. Where was it? It had to be here somewhere…

"I set this to record the new episode of Dark Blood," I said. "Where is it?"

"Ah, that might have been my fault," said Mum, tucking in to her dinner. "Ooh, now this one is spicy!"

"What do you mean, your fault?" I asked.

"There was a thing in the paper about stuff bursting into flames because they've been left plugged in for too long," replied Mum, wafting her hand in front of her mouth. "So I unplugged everything in the house before I went out shopping the other day."

Mark groaned. "That's what happened to the ice cream in the freezer!"

Mum nodded apologetically. "I forgot to plug it all back in when I got home again," she admitted.

I sighed. "So my programme didn't record, then?"

"Sorry," said Mum.

I stood and collected up my dinner boxes.

"Where do you think you're going?" she demanded.

"Upstairs," I said. "I'll have to watch it on catch-up on my computer…"

"No, you're not," said Mum. "You'll sit back down and eat here with us, like a proper family."

I wanted to scream. Wanted to yell at her that we were nothing like a proper family any more. Not since she'd told my Dad not to bother coming home again, that he could go and shack up with 'one of his fancy-women'. But I didn't. I sat back down and swallowed my anger. Like I always did.

So I ate my chicken and chips – which turned out to be very tasty, not that I was about to tell anyone that – while we flicked through TV channels, eventually settling on a quiz show where celebrity contestants none of us recognised had to answer questions to win money for their chosen charities.

By the time the quiz ended, we'd emptied the numerous takeaway boxes and dishes – with the exception of the free garlic bread. That sat balanced on the edge of the table, ponging away.

"Take the boxes out to the bin, Mark," said Mum.

"I'm not going out there," said Mark. "It's pitch black."

"Scared of the dark, are you?" I teased.

"No!" Mark spat. "Next door's dog got through the fence earlier. I don't want to risk standing in whatever it did out there before they came to get it back."

"Alright," said Mum. "Just put the boxes on the side in the kitchen. I'll take them out to the bin in the morning."

"We can't do that," I protested. "They'll stink the house out all night."

"So what do you suggest we do?" asked Mum.

"I'll take the boxes out," I said, throwing Mark an angry look. "I'll just be careful where I'm walking!"

I stood and collected an armful of finished meals, with the garlic bread balanced on top…

… and then the power went out.

CHAPTER 3

DARK

"Aw!" groaned Mark, pointing to the darkened TV. "I was watching that!"

I shook my head in despair. "It was an advert for furniture polish!"

"Yeah, but I haven't seen it before."

Mum was at the window, peering out. "Looks like it's the whole street," she said. "No lights anywhere."

I dumped the boxes on top of Mark as he lay, still stretched out on the sofa. "Make yourself useful,"

I said. "Take these out to the kitchen – for now – and get some candles from under the sink while you're there."

"But, there's no lights…"

"That's why we need the candles, genius!"

"It's dark!"

"You said you weren't scared…"

"I'm not!"

"Then why are you still here?"

Muttering insults under his breath, Mark collected up the boxes and left the room. I slumped back on the sofa, grateful for a comfortable seat at last. My hand hit something hard beside me and I ran my fingers over it. Made of cardboard, about the size of a small pizza box…

The garlic bread!

"You missed one!" I called out to Mark.

"Stick it up your bum!"

"Mark Hagen!" shouted Mum.

"So-rry," Mark called back sarcastically.
He reappeared in the living-room doorway.

"There aren't any candles."

"There are candles," I said. "You're not
looking properly."

"Yes I am!"

"You never do!" I sighed, pushing myself up out
of my seat. "I'll get them…"

Mark made a dash for the sofa as I headed for
the door. I caught his arm. "And I'm sitting there
when I get back!"

"Whatever…"

"Still no lights anywhere," said Mum from the window.

The kitchen was darker than I'd expected. I felt in my pocket for my phone, thinking I could use the screen to light the way, but it wasn't there. I must have left it up in my room.

However, no electricity didn't mean no power… I grabbed a takeaway menu from beneath the cutlery tray in the top drawer – half hoping it was the one for the place where Carlos worked – rolled it into a tube, then lit one of the gas rings on the cooker and held the paper over the flame.

Mini flaming torch acquired, I made for the cupboard beneath the sink as the fire cast dancing shadows all around me…

Then I jumped. Out of the corner of my eye, I spotted someone looking in through the kitchen window from the back garden, their eyes bright. I fought to calm my breath and, heart thudding, I went to see who it was.

I couldn't see anyone. It was probably just the reflection of my tiny flame in the two glass panes of the double-glazing that had looked like flashing eyes… No – hang on, there was someone out there…

I opened the back door to find a chubby man making his way across our back lawn. It was the next-door neighbour. "You haven't seen Pixie, have you?" he asked. "She got through the gap in the fence again."

"Sorry, no," I replied, keeping a close eye on my burning menu. The flame was getting close to my hand.

I closed the door and hurried back to the cupboard, rooting through the bottles of floor cleaner and fabric softener for the candles. I was sure we had some…

The menu had burned out by the time I arrived back in the living room. "We haven't got any candles," I said.

"Ha!" cried Mark. "Told you!"

"Go and boil your head!"

"Sally Hagen!" snapped Mum.

"Well, he's annoying…"

"No more than you were at that age," said Mum. "Now, haven't you got some candles up in your room?"

"Yes, but they're my special ones…"

"What's so special about them?" asked Mark. "They certainly don't keep weirdoes from stalking you."

"That's enough," I warned.

"And now he knows where you live you'll never be able to get rid of him!" Mark giggled. "He'll be forever putt-putting here on his little moped…"

"I said, that's enough!" I lashed out with my fist, determined to give Mark a dead arm to match the dead leg I'd provided him with earlier – but he held up the box of now-cold garlic bread to protect himself. My hand went through the flimsy cardboard and sank into the whiffy garlic butter coating the pizza-crust base.

"Yuck!" I groaned, wiping the goo off on Mark's T-shirt.

"Hey, that stinks!" he cried.

"I know!"

"Sally and Mark Hagen!" Mum shouted. "Stop it, both of you!"

We did. It was easy to tell when we'd gone too far, and this was pretty close.

"You," Mum said to Mark, "clean up that mess; and you…" she turned to me, "go up and get these special candles of yours."

"But they're expensive!"

"I don't care," said Mum. "We're going to use them down here until the power comes back on."

I stuck my tongue out at Mark, then stomped up the stairs to my bedroom. I found the door handle in the dark and slipped inside. There was a light on my bedside table; it was my mobile. I grabbed it and discovered a message – from Carlos...

Great to see you tonight, you looked lovely. Carlos.

I deleted the text and stuffed the phone into my pocket. That was all I needed – Mark being right about him zipping out to see me on his moped all the time. I'd had enough of him trailing round after me at school. If Casey and Jo found out that he knew where I lived, I'd never live it –"

SCREAM!

I jumped at the sound. It had come from outside. What was it? A cat? Kids messing about?

No, that couldn't be right. It had hardly sounded human…

I hurried to the window and peered out at the dark garden below. I could just make out a large shape lying in the middle of the lawn. I laughed. It was the bloke from next door! He'd probably slipped in a pile of poo left behind by his precious dog! Great scream, though. He could have a good career doing voice-overs for little girls in films!

I felt guilty for laughing and decided that helping him find his lost dog would be the neighbourly thing to do. So I grabbed my expensive purple candles and hurried downstairs. I opened the back door to find him still lying there on the grass.

I was suddenly worried. What if he'd banged his head on something when he fell? Would we be responsible? Could he sue us? That would be all we needed.

I pulled my phone from my pocket and switched it on, using the dim light to pick my way across the lawn towards my unmoving neighbour – being careful not to stand in any of his precious Pixie's little presents myself.

"Tom…" I said, "are you OK?"

Tom's eyes were open – wide and staring – but he didn't reply. My mobile lit up a dark stain on his neck. It seemed to glisten a deep purple colour. I moved the phone lower – and froze. His entire throat was missing.

It looked as though it had been torn away, as if by some crazed animal. The skin was ragged at the sides, the windpipe was gone and I could see the white bone of his spine, deep inside the wound. The dark purple liquid was blood, pooling on the grass and soaking into the toes of my trainers.

That's when I heard the sound – a kind of wheezing hiss coming from behind the trampoline at the end of the garden. Maybe it was Tom's dog, hurt like her master. Pushing away the urge to flee, I held my phone out in trembling fingers and made my way around the bloodied corpse of my neighbour.

"H-hello?" I called quietly, hoping I wouldn't get a reply. "Is there someone there? Pixie, is that you?"

Something shifted in the dark and I heard the hiss again. I turned my phone towards the sound and felt my stomach flip over.

A thin figure was crouched near the wall at the end of the garden, something small and hairy clutched in its long-nailed fingers and blood pouring down its chin. Its eyes flickered up to look at me – bright, orange, burning – then it went back to noisily eating what was left of Pixie, tearing lumps out of the dog with two sharp, white teeth.

I felt my blood run cold and my body begin to shake as I stumbled back towards the house, not wanting to believe what I had just seen.

It was a vampire.

CHAPTER 4

DEFENCE

I slammed and bolted the kitchen door, then ran for the living room. "Don't go outside!" I sobbed. "Don't either of you go outside!"

But neither Mum nor Mark seemed to hear me. They were staring at the figure pressed against the glass of the living-room window. Another vampire.

The creature had ghastly, white skin – like an uncooked chicken – and eyes that flashed orange with every glance around the room. Its hands, pressed against the window, ended in long, razor-sharp nails – each tainted yellow and tipped with dried blood.

"Cool!" said Mark, making for the window.

I grabbed the collar of his T-shirt and pulled him back. "No!" I cried. "It is NOT cool – it's a monster!"

"Oh, don't be such a killjoy!" said Mum with a grin. "It's just some kids trick-or-treating."

"But it's weeks until Halloween!" I protested.

"So they're practising."

I led Mum back to where Mark was standing and pulled the curtains closed. "Listen to me," I said. "You're not going to believe this, but we're being attacked by vampires!"

"You're right," said Mark, "I don't believe you."

I spun him round to face me. "They've just eaten Tom and his dog – in our back garden!"

Mark frowned. "Don't be daft!"

"Do you want me to show you?"

"Yeah, OK…"

"It's not nice…"

"I don't care!"

I took Mark's arm and steered him towards the living-room door. He pulled back. "Is it… bad?"

I nodded. "Very. There's not much left."

Mark shuddered. "I don't want to see it."

I wrapped him in my arms. "I know you don't," I said. "I wasn't really going to show you."

"We don't have any sweets in yet!" said my Mum's voice slowly and loudly. Mark and I turned to discover she had opened the curtains to address the vampire – no, strike that – dozen or more vampires gathered on the front lawn.

The creature at the front was scratching at the glass with one of his yellow talons, scoring a circle in the space between himself and Mum.

"They are good, aren't they?" said Mum, appreciatively. "Last year it was all toilet paper mummies, and werewolves made out of carpet cut-offs – but this lot have really gone to town with their costumes."

The circle of glass described by the vampire's nail shattered into a dozen pieces. Now there was only the inner pane separating us from a garden full of ravenous monsters.

Mark and I pulled Mum back across the room to the sofa and sat either side of her, holding her arms.

"What are we going to do?" my brother cried.

"How would I know?" I replied.

"You're the one who goes around dressed like a creature of the night," said Mark. "Can't you just go and – I dunno – talk to them?"

I stared at him. "And say what? 'Excuse me, I see you like to dress in black like me – is there any way you could possibly avoid eating my family because we have a similar taste in fashion?'"

"There's no need to be sarcastic!"

More screams rang out from outside. Mark and I glanced up at the window. More vampires were roaming the street now, several of them dragging the limp, bloodied body of one of our neighbours behind them.

"Ooh, look – that's Mrs Wright from number fifteen," said Mum, standing to get a better look. "She always does like to join in the fun at Halloween…"

I pulled Mum back into her seat and tried to ignore the piercing squeal of nail against window.

Our vampire was still scratching into the inner pane of glass.

"I'm not being sarcastic!" I hissed to Mark. "I'm scared!"

"Me, too," said Mark. "And a little bit excited. Vampires are real, Sally!"

"And that excites you?"

"Yes! All these years I've been watching movies and reading comic books – and now they're here!"

I pointed to the creature creating a hole in our living-room window, "And they're breaking into our house!"

"Don't worry," said Mark. "He can't fit through a small hole like that…"

I paused for a second, uncertain what to say next. Mark was right. The vampire was cutting a hole no bigger than a dinner plate. It was far too small even for a small child to squeeze through.

"Unless he turns himself into a bat and flies in, or just reaches in and undoes the lock," Mark added.

I jumped up off the sofa. "Quick!" I shouted. "Grab the other end of the TV!"

"Why?" Mark asked.

"So we can ram it up against the window!"

"You want to show the vampires some TV?" said Mark with a frown. "How will you know which channel they prefer?"

"No, you idiot…"

"Sally Hagen!" chided Mum.

I ignored her. "We're going to use the TV to block the hole in the window and stop that thing getting inside."

Mark stood and crossed the room to help me. "Alright," he said, "but you're wasting your time."

"Saving our lives is a waste of time?"

Mark shrugged. "One: if the vampire's nails can cut through a double-glazed window, then a cheap, supermarket-brand flat-screen TV isn't going to be much of a challenge. And, two: he can't come inside, even if he takes the whole window out."

I blinked. "Why not?"

Mark sighed, as though the answer was obvious. "He's a vampire!" he said. "He can't cross the threshold without our permission. You have to invite him in!"

Of course! Mark was right! If vampires were suddenly real – then all the rules associated with vampires were real as well…

They can't enter a house without being invited…

They can be killed with a wooden stake to the heart…

Crosses and holy water can repel them…

And so can garlic!

Mark and I smiled at each other, then made a dive for the box of free, cold garlic bread sitting next to Mum on the sofa. We tore open the already damaged lid and grabbed a slice each.

"Go on!" said Mark. "Try it…"

Cautiously approaching the window, I began to smear the slice of garlic bread on the glass around the hole the vampire was cutting. The effect was instant, the creature screamed as though burned and shrank away, spitting angrily.

"It works!" I grinned, giving Mark a greasy high-five.

There was another scream from outside – a child's scream this time. Mark pressed his face to the window and peered down the street in the moonlight. "Tim and Sasha, the twins at number nine," he said, turning away, his cheeks pale.

"But how?" I asked. "We know the garlic has an effect, so the other rules – like inviting them over the threshold – should work, too."

Mark could only shrug. "I don't know…"

"I think I've got some mints in my bedside cabinet," said Mum, standing up again. "Do you think mints count as sweets?"

Mark and I were sitting her down again, when…

CRASH!

The noise came from the direction of the kitchen. "The vampire in the garden!" I exclaimed. I grabbed another couple of slices of garlic bread and pulled open the living-room door. "Stay in here, and keep Mum with you!" I ordered.

I ran down the hallway and into the darkened kitchen. The first vampire I'd seen had obviously finished with his doggy treat, and was hammering at the back door, trying to break it open.

"No, you don't!" I yelled, hurling garlic bread at the glass in the door. The vampire screamed and backed away. I smeared the stinking butter all over the door, then wiped my hands on my jeans and turned to go back to Mum and Mark.

A cold breeze hit me and I looked up to see the front door was wide open.

"Hello again, Sally," said a voice from behind me.

CHAPTER 5

DANGER

I spun round, knowing I'd heard that voice before.

The figure behind me in the kitchen was tall and slim. Dressed in a sharp, black suit and long, leather coat, his ebony hair was swept back above chiselled, white features. Blood-red lips parted in a cold smile, revealing two long, pointed fangs.

He looked so different from the last time I'd seen him, but it was definitely the same guy...

"Carlos!" I gasped.

Carlos's eyes flashed orange. "I was hoping to see you again soon," he soothed. "I hadn't planned for it to be tonight, but my cousins were getting hungry."

I glanced back at the open front door. "How did you get inside?" I demanded. "I thought you had to be –"

"– Invited?" The vampire took a step towards me. "Oh, but you did invite me – or, rather, your lovely mother did earlier this evening when I asked to use the toilet."

I shuddered as another scream rang out in the night. Another of my neighbours was being attacked. "The other houses…"

Carlos nodded. "I've delivered to everyone around here at one time or another – takeaways, parcels, groceries… and it's amazing how quick they all are to invite pathetic little Carlos in when he needs a glass of water, or to use the phone. Once I'm inside, it's quick work to invite my family to join me."

"You're attacking innocent people!" I cried. "Killing them!"

Carlos raised a long-nailed finger to wag at me. "Not all of them," he said. "Some of them have been chosen to join our clan. Those adorable twins from down the street will make fine servants for my throne room."

"You monster!" I lashed out with my hand and slapped him hard across the cheek. My palm came away covered in ice. I shivered.

"Now, now…" teased Carlos, stepping towards me again. "It's one thing to hurt my feelings by repeatedly refusing my invitations to the school prom – but I would never have thought you were the type to resort to physical violence."

I pushed my freezing hand into my pocket and clutched the piece of garlic bread waiting there. "If you come anywhere near my family, I'll kill you!"

"How?" Carlos chuckled. "With the garlic bread you got free with your very unhealthy dinner? Think about who delivered it, Sally... Unlike my cousins, I've built up quite a tolerance towards the stuff."

I pulled my hand out of my pocket.

"There's a good girl..." Carlos smiled. "Now, if you'd be so good as to step aside, I'd like to drink from your mother and brother. I think I'll take the child first – the blood of the young is so full of vitality, it almost fizzes!"

He took another step forwards – so I kicked him as hard as I could between his legs with the pointed toe of my shoe. Vampire or no vampire – there's one attack that no man can build up a tolerance to!

Carlos collapsed to the kitchen floor in agony. "You'll die for this!" he whined.

I turned and raced back towards the living room.

Carlos half-ran, half-stumbled after me. I'd just made it to the door when he grabbed my ankle with his icy hands. I felt my skin burn with the cold.

I fell and kicked out with my other foot, but he was ready for me this time. He grasped my other ankle and began to drag himself towards me. I screamed and heard the living-room door open. Mark was peering out at me, eyes wide. "Get back inside!" I shouted.

"Do as your sister says!" said Carlos, crawling closer. "It will be your turn soon enough, little boy…"

The door slammed shut again.

Whether it would be effective or not, I pulled the piece of garlic bread from my pocket and threw it at my attacker. It landed with a SLAP against Carlos's cheek, and I heard the stinging HISS as it burned his skin. He tore it away and glared at me with those flashing, orange eyes.

"I've changed my mind!" he snarled, dragging himself along my body. "I'll take you first – and leave the boy until last, so he can watch me and my family devour your mother…"

The vampire opened his mouth, his fangs glistening.

"Wait!" I cried.

Carlos paused in his advance. "Yes?"

"What about if I agree to go to the prom with you?"

The vampire smiled, licking the tips of his fangs. "The school prom?"

I nodded. "We'll go together – like a date. Boyfriend and girlfriend. Just like you've been asking."

"That's cute," Carlos smiled.

I risked a smile of my own. "Really?"

"Of course!"

"You mean you like the idea?"

"I love it!" beamed Carlos. "But, there is one tiny, little problem…"

My smile faded away. "What?"

The vampire gestured to the front door. I turned to see one of his cousins crossing our lawn, a human head gripped in its talons. I closed my eyes before I could recognise which of the residents of our street it used to be. "I think we're a little way past school proms now, don't you, Sally?"

"Wh-what do you mean?"

"It's a new world!" Carlos enthused. "A world where my kind no longer have to hide away in the shadows and see ourselves ridiculed in books and movies." He spat a glob of green phlegm onto the wall beside me. I watched as it began to slide down towards the floor. "Sparkling in the sunshine, indeed!"

Then his eyes flashed and he focused on me once more. "But, with a few tweaks, we could make your idea work…"

I swallowed hard. "How?"

Carlos smiled. "Just bite and you become one of us. A beautiful vampire! You can sit by my side as my Queen for all eternity!"

I sneered. "Bog off, funny fangs!"

"Sally Hagen!" shouted Mum through the wall.

Carlos hissed angrily and lunged towards me, teeth bared.

Suddenly, the living-room door flew open again and Mark jumped out into the hallway. He had a piece of garlic bread dangling on a length of curtain cord around his neck – and two pencils in his hands, making the shape of a cross.

"Begone, foul beast!" he roared.

Carlos halted his attack – but only to laugh. The sound started as a chilling chuckle, then quickly became a raucous guffaw. "You... you think you can make a crucifix out of just anything?" he cried. He let go of me and pushed himself up onto his knees, hands raised in mock terror. "Oh, who will save me from the little brat armed with the contents of his school pencil-case?"

Mark's expression darkened. "No one!" he yelled, leaping over me towards the vampire. Before I could stop him, he raised one of the pencils high in the air, then brought it down hard, stabbing it deep into Carlos's right eye.

CHAPTER 6

DEAL

Carlos's eyeball popped, then the vampire fell back screaming in pain and clutching at his face. Mark dragged me back into the living room. We slammed the door closed and fell against it, struggling to catch our breath. Out in the hallway, we could hear Carlos wailing like a wild animal and thrashing about.

"Quick!" I said to Mark. "The sofa…"

We shifted Mum back into her armchair and dragged the sofa across the room, pressing it up against the door just as the handle began to rattle.

"Come out, Sally!" called Carlos. "I want to talk to you!"

"What about?" I shouted back.

"I want to make you a deal," said Carlos. "Just come out into the hallway and we can discuss it."

"Anything you've got to say to me, you can say it from there!"

I heard Carlos sigh. "Alright," he said. "Your brother has caused me a lot of pain…"

"Good!" yelled Mark.

Carlos hissed. "Give him to me and I'll let you and your mother live."

"Chuff off, ugly!" bellowed Mum.

Mark and I stared at her in surprise. "Anna Hagen!" I exclaimed.

"Well," said Mum, "what did you expect me to say?" She smiled sadly at us. "It's all real, isn't it?"

"I'm afraid so," I said. Mark hurried over to hug her.

"I think you've got your answer..." I shouted through the door.

"Then you will rue the day you were ever born!"

Footsteps stomped away towards the kitchen and then there was silence.

"OK," I said. "Mark – check the radio. That's got batteries, so it will still work. See if this is on the news. We need to find out if this is just happening locally, or if it's everywhere."

Mark nodded and grabbed the old radio from the sideboard.

"Mum," I said, "we have to block up the broken window."

"What with?"

"The table," I said, sweeping the piles of clothes to the floor.

"I've just washed that lot!" Mum moaned.

Ignoring her complaints, I tipped the table onto its side and struggled to lift it up. Reluctantly, she took the other end and we hefted the table up and wedged it into the window frame. It took a few kicks and shoulder charges to get it in there firmly – and the plasterwork on the walls either side would never be quite the same again – but we eventually got it to stay in place.

"Nothing," said Mark, looking up from the radio. "Just static. All the stations are off-air."

I nodded. "It's everywhere, then."

"The whole world?"

"Could be," I said. "Have you still got your penknife?"

Mark pulled the knife from his pocket and handed it over.

"I thought I told you to get rid of that thing!" Mum exclaimed.

"It's lucky for us he didn't," I said.

"Why?" asked Mum. "What are we going to do?"

I flipped a dining chair onto its side and stamped on one of its legs until it snapped off. I snatched up the broken length of wood and studied the jagged end.

"Watch and see…"

*

An hour later, I pulled the sofa away from the living-room door and crept out into the hallway. It was empty, but I could hear movement coming from the kitchen.

"Carlos!" I called. "Are you there?"

The vampire appeared in the kitchen doorway, a deep hole where his right eye should have been. Dark, almost black, blood had run down his face and dried there.

"What do you want?"

"I've been thinking about your deal," I said.

Carlos looked me up and down. I'd reapplied my scarlet lipstick, darkened my purple eye-shadow and painted my fingernails black. I looked good, and he knew it.

"Which deal?"

"The one about my brother," I said, reaching inside the living-room door. I pulled Mark out into the hallway with me. His hands were tied behind his back and he was crying. "Will you let Mum live if I hand him over?"

"Please…" sobbed Mark. "Please don't do this!"

Carlos took a step towards us. "You mean it?"

I looked down at my little brother in contempt. "You haven't been stuck in the same room as the little monster all night," I said. "I'll be glad to get rid of him if only to stop the stink of his farts."

Carlos half-smiled. "Slugs and snails and puppy-dog tails… That's what little boys are made of."

I shoved Mark down the hallway towards him and laughed. "Take a bite and see for yourself…"

The vampire approached my brother, who turned and started to run back. "Sally! Please!" he blubbed.

I produced the knife and Mark stopped on the spot. As did Carlos.

"What's that for?" he demanded.

I smiled. "An experiment…" Clutching Mark's chin in my free hand, I ran the tip of the knife blade down his cheek, producing a thin line of blood. Then, not shifting my gaze from Carlos's flashing, orange stare, I bent and licked the blood from my brother's face, making sure the crimson fluid smeared across my lips.

I heard Carlos gasp as I stood and took a deep breath. "I want the other deal, as well,"

I breathed heavily. "The one where I live forever as your Queen…"

Carlos strode down the hallway towards me and took me in his strong arms. He pushed his lips against mine, and I felt his ice-cold tongue explore the inside of my mouth…

…where it found the last remaining slice of cold garlic bread hidden inside my cheek. I used my own tongue to push it deep inside his throat.

The vampire staggered back against the wall, his lips beginning to blister and crack. "What have you done?" he demanded.

"I've been thinking!" I said, my hand gripping his neck. "You may have developed a tolerance to garlic on the outside, but I bet your insides are just as sensitive – and do you know what? It looks like I was right!"

"I'll kill you for this!" Carlos wheezed through his injured mouth.

"I doubt it!" I snarled.

Mum appeared in the living-room doorway and tossed one of the broken dining-chair legs to me – its tip whittled to a razor-sharp point. I caught the stick deftly and spun it in my fingers.

"Time for me to make a delivery of my own!" I grunted, then I rammed the stake hard into Carlos's chest, piercing his heart.

The vampire opened his mouth to scream – but disappeared in a cloud of dust before he could make a sound.

Mark freed his hands from the slipknot holding them behind his back. "I really thought you were going to side with him for a minute there," he said, wiping the blood from his cheek.

"Sorry," I said, ruffling his hair, "but I had to sound convincing."

"It will be dawn soon," said Mum, gathering the other stakes we'd made from chair legs and tying them together with the last of the curtain cord.

"We'll wait until it's light, then we should be safe to get to the car," I said.

"Where are we going to go?" asked Mark.

I shrugged. "The church first, I suppose. We can stock up on holy water and crosses that will have a real effect on these things."

"And then?" said Mum.

I ran the polished toe of my shoe through the pile of dust that used to be Carlos. "Then we find other people who survived tonight," I said, "and we start to fight back…"

THE END